Lady Bug

IP

ITHACA PRESS

NEW YORK

Ithaca Press
3 Kimberly Drive, Suite B
Dryden, New York 13053 USA
www.IthacaPress.com

Book Design by Gary Marsden

Illustrations by Kip Herring

Manufactured in the United States of America

9   8   7   6   5   4   3   2   1

Library of Congress Cataloging-in-Publication Data is available

Stone/ Jodi
Children's fiction

First Edition

ISBN 0-9754298-7-6

www.JodiStone.com

Lady Bug

By Jodi Stone

Illustrated by Kip Herring

Dedication

Ladybug

A story written in honor of a little boy whose time
here on earth was cut too short.

Jace Stephen Stone

September 29,1997- May 18, 2003

Acknowledgements

Thank you

I lost my beautiful little boy Jace and Bryan the father of my two children in a car accident.

Jace was only five years old.

He loved ladybugs.

He loved to paint and draw pictures.

He loved to pick flowers and give them to everyone along with a big smile and hug.

Jace also loved very much his big brother Slater, my surviving son.

This story was inspired by Jace and is in loving memory of him.

It is dedicated to Slater my beautiful son, my strength to carry on.

Slater you are an amazing little boy.

You have such a big heart.

Never stop reaching for the stars.

I love you to the moon and back.

I would like to thank all the people at MADD (Mothers against drunk driving).

MADD is a wonderful organization with people who are there and who care.

Jace and Bryan were not killed by a drunk driver but the people at MADD have helped me in so many ways just by simply being there for me.

Lady Bug on the
pretty flower,
Come play with me.

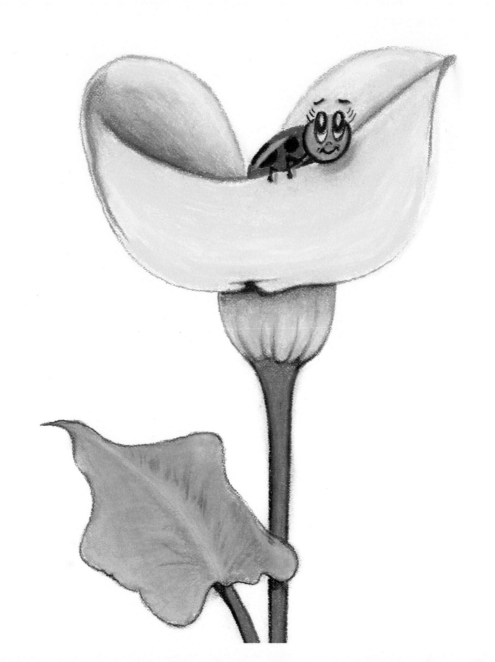

Lady Bug on my toe,
Crawling up
to my knee.

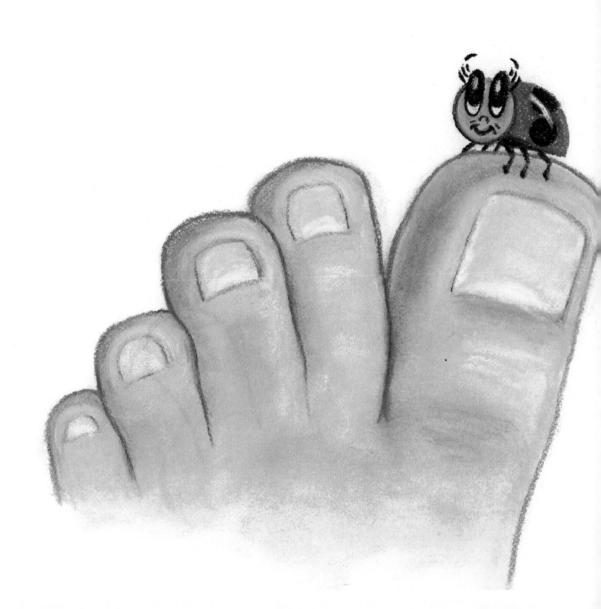

Lady Bug on my tummy,

That tickles

and feels funny.

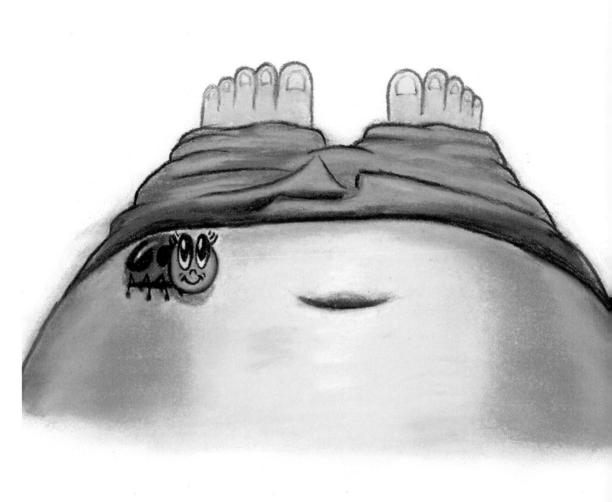

Lady Bug on my shoulder,

Be careful not to

fall over.

Lady Bug on my nose,

I wonder

where she goes.

Lady Bug on the tree,
Come sit back
on my knee.

Lady Bug has one, two, three, four spots.
Lady bug, you fly high and free.

On the tip of my finger,
Come inside and meet
my mother.

Lady bug, time to go outside and fly away.

Please come again and play with me some day.

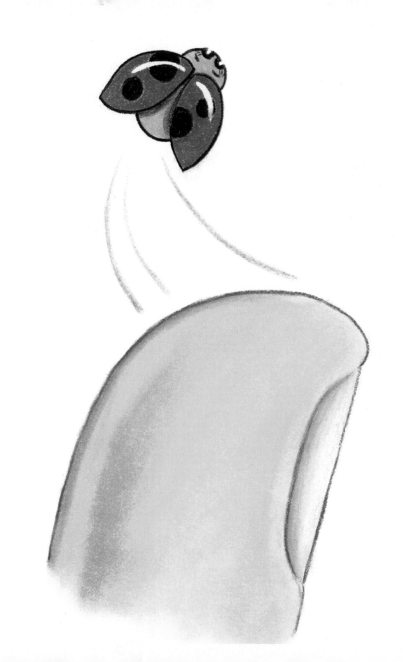

About the Author

Jodi Stone is a single mom who finds great joy in raising her son Slater. She was inspired to write this book in memory of her son Jace, who loved lady bugs.

Jodi and Slater live in North Central Texas.

About the Illustrator

Kip Herring is an award-winning artist who exhibits his talent through a variety of artistic mediums. Kip expresses his mastery of aesthetic vision in each painting he renders.

The art in Lady Bug shows his unique and whimsical style and adds to enhances the text of this lovely little book.